Wraith

By Tim Maddox

First Published in Print 04/17/2026

First Published 10/01/2025 (Sally Port Magazine)

Books by Tim Maddox:

Standalones:
Forest Flight (2020)
In The Reeds (2024)

Fairy Tale Adaptations:
The Tale of Snow White and Rose Red (2025)

The Hammer of Fate series:
Alone Among Stars (2026)

Wraith series:
Wraith (2026)

Wraith

By Tim Maddox

First Published in Print 04/17/2026

First Published 10/01/2025 (Sally Port Magazine)

Wraith was originally published in Sally Port Magazine in their October 2025 issue.

Cover design: Ehsan221b

Typeset: Garamontio (all text)

Author website: www.timmaddoxbooks.com

Social media: @TimMaddoxAuthor on X/Twitter
                       Tim Maddox, Author on Facebook
                       TimMaddoxAuthor on Instagram

ISBNs: 979-8-9921954-6-0 (paperback)
                       979-8-9921954-7-7 (ebook)

Table of Contents:

Part 1:

First Signs

The golden sunset greeted Aeron Duskling as his horse trotted through the unfamiliar forests. They'd had a long ride from the Bicorun River, but Snowstorm was a credit to her Cambrian sires. Aeron guessed that they had traveled over fifty miles their crossing this morning, and it was another hundred beyond that to the battle lines around the Dreadfort.

Just that thought alone caused Aeron to exhale. For three years he'd been looking over his shoulders, aware that death could come at a moment's notice. Now, he might finally get to let down his guard.

Aeron shook his head. *As if I could ever do that while the Wraiths are still hunting me.*

Sighing, he looked to the distant hills. He remembered the broken peak to the north from the maps Grand Master Reylund had shown him. From here, he needed to continue southwest and find the road into the heartlands of Arca. Once inside the guardian hills, it would only be a day or so until Snowstorm carried him to the Citadel to undertake the rites of a Sun Guard Master.

I might finally get a good night's rest. He reached down and patted the mare's neck. "I'd say you made a solid sixty miles today, old girl."

Snowstorm bobbed her head in reply. Aeron chuckled, then took a deep breath of the late autumn air.

The faint scent of death and smoke struck his nose. At first, Aeron thought it was an unwanted memory, an expected smell that had been a constant companion since the war started five years ago at the Battle of Redwood. He took another breath, and the scent remained. It was coming from the direction of the broken peak.

There shouldn't be any fighting this far from the river. Aeron's thoughts went first to bandits, but his instincts didn't agree. He turned Snowstorm north and rode toward the scent.

Darkness had fully set in when they finally reached the smoldering village, the aethereal currents filled with a familiar dark magic. The hair on the back of Aeron's neck stood on end. *Wraiths, here?!*

Just knowing he was near the cult warriors put Aeron on alert. He instinctively cast several spells. The first suppressed his aura, allowing him to be undetected by any lingering Wraiths. Following that, he cast a pair of glamors; the weaker glamor changed his appearance to that of a simple traveler, while the stronger glamor cloaked his two swords from view. Both types of spells were difficult techniques to learn, but he had spent years perfecting them out of necessity.

Dismounting Snowstorm, Aeron studied the carnage with both hands hovering over the cloaked hilts of his swords, ready in case someone returned to find him.

He found that six trails had emerged from the eastern tree line. The buildings on that side had caught fire first, and there was no sign of any opposition to the attack. From experience, he knew to circle to the other side of the village to avoid the carnage within. He found a cluster of women, children, and elderly laying at the edge of the buildings. There were two new trails here, trails that moved deliberately and seemed to have been unnoticed by the villagers.

Flankers. They must have waited until the survivors tried to flee together.

Fifty yards beyond the ruins lay the bodies of the fighting men of the village. Among them, Aeron could see a dozen soldiers wearing the sigil of the Kingdom of Rigia and a single heap of blackened ash where the villagers had slain a Wraith. Further study revealed that the men had been returning to the village when the entire force from Rigia had descended upon them. Aeron was certain that if he followed the men's tracks, he would find the signs of an initial engagement where the villagers had appeared to be victorious.

A perfect Wraith ambush, aside from one of their own dying. Aeron surveyed the final stand closely, hoping to learn as much as he could about the strength of his foes. *If this was a full raiding company, there are still eleven Wraiths, with perhaps a hundred soldiers supporting them.*

The sight alarmed Aeron. Even in the early days of the war, when the Sun Guards had taken defeat after defeat, the Wraiths had never entered the forests beyond the Bicorun. He knew that for certain.

This raid was an act of desperation, and it held the potential to throw everything Arca had achieved into question. If these Wraiths penetrated the heartland of the kingdom and gained acolytes, Arca would have to move troops back in order to hunt them down. That would lead to the frontline armies being weaker, helping the Wraiths and Rigia.

It may even turn the tide back in Rigia's favor. Aeron shook his head and turned back to Snowstorm. *Seems I can never escape them.*

Swinging into the saddle, Aeron consulted his memory of Arca's maps. Because of the rugged hills, the next village along the Rigians' line of advance lay some ten miles beyond where he was, inside of Arca's original borders. This would mark the first time that Wraiths had entered the heartland since the founding of the Sun Guards. Rigia's force, although small, would have fertile grounds to sow fear and destruction should they get beyond that village.

Not on my life. Aeron touched his heels to Snowstorm's ribs and turned into the woods.

There was little hope he could reach the next village during the night. The course he chose had no roads in order to avoid detection by the Wraiths. Nor did Aeron worry about whether the Wraiths had already reached the next village. The custom of their order was to celebrate following a successful raid, and Aeron knew it had been over a year since they had executed a raid worth celebrating. He and the other Sun Guards had seen to that.

If the Wraiths will risk twelve of their number on such a mission, how many children have they stolen from Rigia to fill their ranks?

Aeron shook his head. *Worries for after tomorrow, and after I've passed my rites.* He reached down and patted Snowstorm's neck. "A little further today, old girl, then we can rest."

The Cambrian nodded and trotted through the forest. Aeron took care to guide Snowstorm toward the harsh hillsides, hoping his foes had chosen the easier valleys as their path into the heartland.

Two hours passed before Snowstorm reached the end of her endurance and stood still in a small clearing with a gnarled oak at its center. Aeron dismounted and led Snowstorm to the tree. Once there, she immediately laid down and took several large breaths.

"You and me both." Aeron told the horse as he petted her neck. He then glanced around to see if there were any deadfalls to make a fire with.

He felt a pulse from the black sword at his hip just as a faint shimmer among the trees caught his attention. Instinctively, Aeron continued to pet Snowstorm while keeping watch out of the corner of his eye. For a while there was nothing, then the shimmer appeared again, closer this time.

A cloaked Wraith.

Aeron sighed, grinning sadly at their luck as he channeled a cloaking glamor. He leaned down to Snowstorm and whispered, "Guess we're not resting here tonight, either." Aeron then stepped around the tree as he loosed the glamor. The moment he was back in view, he began running just to the left of the shimmer.

As Aeron expected, the Wraith stopped in their tracks, then ducked down behind a bush, apprehensively trying to locate him.

The distance closed swiftly. The lack of movement by the Wraith told Aeron two things; first, that his own cloaking glamor was working perfectly; and second, that the Wraith was inexperienced. One of the first lessons taught to a Sun Guard was that if an opponent disappeared like Aeron had just done, you were to retreat immediately. If nothing else, get out of the open. Even most Wraiths, despite the oddity of a Sun Guard being capable of casting such a glamor, knew to be cautious of their techniques being turned against them.

His foe was still facing toward Snowstorm. Aeron could feel the nervous energy of his opponent. It was an energy he was intimately familiar with. The sensation of the hunter becoming the hunted. His old battle fever awakened at the energy.

Aeron slipped behind the Wraith and made one last check of the aethereal currents. *It's just us.* The fever cleared as he reached for the hilt of the dagger on his right hip and slid it about a finger's width from its sheath. "You don't have to die tonight," he said calmly as his glamors vanished due to the dagger's magic.

The Wraith gasped and wheeled around, her own cloaking glamor fading as the shock broke her concentration. Her voice was youthful, but the raven-like mask concealed any other features besides her long blonde hair and startled green eyes. The large mask told of her inexperience; as a Wraith gained notoriety, the masks would be cut away piece by piece until only the part around the eyes remained. Micalus' renown was such that he wore no mask at all, even after he became the Grand Inquisitor.

The main exception to this custom were the other Inquisitors—their white masks were terrifying, especially when they appeared as a disembodied head in the dark. Seeing that mask meant you were facing the best of the Wraiths.

"Leave the Wraiths behind and come with me," Aeron offered his free hand toward her. "You will be safe inside Arca."

For a moment, it looked like she would accept. Then her eyes took on a red hue. A smoky aura started forming around her as she reached for her ritual dagger.

That was as far as she got. Aeron flipped his dagger from its sheath and sent it flying. It dispelled her protective aura instantly and buried itself deep into her chest. She dropped her gaze to the wound in disbelief, then looked up at Aeron.

Aeron looked right into her scared eyes. "I'm sorry," he said. The Wraith then collapsed into a pile of blackened ash, leaving her armor and blades behind.

He stood over the pile for a moment. Aeron had seen many Wraiths die and wither to ash, but it was always bittersweet to cut down such a young apprentice. The old masters had decades of crimes to their names, but the young ones, like her, were as innocent as any of their kind could be.

Even then, most people would consider the initiation rites heinous.

He picked up his dagger and turned it over in his hand. A series of white lights crossed the dark aethereal purple of the blade, almost like stars in the night sky. Aeron examined the blade and soon found the new star. She was paler than all the others. The Wraith must have only just completed her initiation before this mission, before the dagger stole her life force.

Sighing, he searched for another star. This one was unique among the other stars in his dagger, in that the white light faded first to gold rather than directly into the aethereal purple. It belonged to Seinya, the first Wraith he had tried to help defect from The Wraith Order. Another cultist had killed her almost immediately when she made her choice. Though Aeron had slain her killer, that knowledge provided little comfort now, nearly three years later. Her life force, her soul, remained trapped in the dagger like all the other souls traversing its blade.

Shaking his head, Aeron sheathed the dagger and gathered the Wraith's gear. Everything the cultists carried was bound to their life force, so when a Wraith fell, only ash remained. There were a few methods which could prevent this, but using one of the ritual daggers was the only one that worked without fail. If her comrades found her gear still intact, they would know Aeron was nearby.

Aeron cast a quick spell, and the silvery halo of his shadow vault opened. Inside were many sets of Wraith gear, all of which he had gained through skill of arms. The scholars at the Citadel were waiting for them, hopeful that they could learn new techniques to combat the cult by studying them. He added her gear to the collection.

The last of the Wraith's gear that Aeron held was her dagger. Despite knowing what he'd find, he unsheathed it. The blade's aethereal glow contained no stars. Wraiths did not slay other Wraiths except under exceptional circumstances; practically all involved treason and betrayal of their Order and the Kingdom of Rigia.

He'd only known two who had betrayed the Wraiths in his lifetime and fled toward Arca; one had died soon after Aeron had met them. As far as Aeron knew, less than a handful throughout all of time had ever escaped to live out some semblance of a life. Seinya had been on the verge of joining that number, and three golden-edged stars held within another dagger had been on a similar journey before they too had fallen to their comrades.

For Aeron, these daggers were his most prized possessions. They held the promise of redemption. If the clerics could sever the corruption from a Wraith's gear, cleansing a Wraith from their ritualistic corruption would also become possible. Seinya's body was already ashes, but perhaps her soul and the others in the daggers could have peace beyond their death. If not, it may still be possible to save a living Wraith before death found them.

If that reality existed, then there could be one less evil in the world.

Aeron smiled sadly. Few would even consider trying to redeem their kind, given the centuries of horrors told around gloomy fires. But then, few knew them like Aeron did. *How many have to die before it's over? How many will I have to kill to save the innocent before I find that salvation?*

Is it even possible?

He held the empty dagger for a few seconds longer. A stray thought considered keeping this dagger at his side since using it wouldn't interfere with his glamors; only his dagger would dispel his magic since Aeron had bonded to it.

The thought was fleeting. One innocuous mistake and the blade would absorb his life force without hesitation. He placed the dagger into the shadow vault, restored his glamors, then led Snowstorm further into the forest.

It was an hour later when the two finally stopped walking and settled down in a hidden glen. Aeron strengthened the detection magic within his black blade, but he still slept lightly in case Rigian scouts happened upon him while the rest of the raiders celebrated.

Enjoy your victory. It will be your last.

Part 2:

Preparations

When dawn kissed the sky, Aeron rose from his faint dreams. Today was a day of singing swords and deadly mistakes; he could feel it in his bones. His old battle fever rose at the notion, though he quelled it. A Sun Guard master shouldn't feed on such emotions. That was the way of the Wraiths.

Snowstorm jumped up the moment Aeron reached his feet. Aeron knew from her stance that she was exhausted, but the Cambrian mare matched his doggedness in every respect. He patted her as he picked up her reins. "Ready to move, old girl?"

Soon after, he swung into the saddle and the pair pushed deeper into the unfamiliar forest.

A long morning passed, as did most of the afternoon. These hills were not like those east of the Miras, which Aeron was intimately familiar with. These had a carpet of flora which seemed determined to never grant passage without a fight. *I know now why Master Reylund told me to take the road; then again, no one would expect an army to march through this.*

Finally, they broke through into a cleared hillside where he could see the flatlands beyond. Aeron took a moment to enjoy the sight. The harvests were just coming in, with many fields golden with grain and only a few patches of browning aftermath. Stands of trees dotted the land, with waterways coursing south toward the crown city and the Citadel. *Arca really is beautiful.*

Exhaling with a smile, Aeron searched the scene until he'd located the nearest village. It was far from the others, maybe a day's walk if one had long legs. That would be the one the Wraiths struck next.

I have to stop them, but the village is too small to have a sufficient fighting force. Except... There was a fortification just beyond it to the northwest. His heart leapt at the sight. *A Sun Guard garrison!* Perhaps that force was powerful enough to hold off the advance.

Though, maybe it wasn't, and that was why the Wraiths were heading toward it. Aeron could see the plan take shape in front of him. Slaughter all the inhabitants of the village and the fort, except for those who their dark magic called to, then use the fort and the ungathered harvest as a base from which to raid from within Arca.

Cold fury filled his veins. He spurred Snowstorm, and she broke into a full gallop.

The fort lay on the other side of the village from him, so Aeron rode into the village first. What he saw gave him pause. Womenfolk were meandering around in apprehensive manners, but aside from a few boys in the fields, he didn't see any men. Even as he rode through the village to the stable, he only saw a few old faces.

A middle-aged stablewoman was standing beside a one-legged elder, their conversation interrupted by Aeron's appearance. Aeron rode up to them and swung out of the saddle. "Where are all your men?"

"Gone," the stablewoman said as she reached out for the reins. "A hunter arrived this morning with word that he'd seen a company of Wraiths and Rigians crossing the hills. Captain Gaheris took the garrison and marched off to face them before they could split up and ravage the land."

"I must have missed them crossing over the hills." Aeron replied with a sigh. "They destroyed the village east of here. I was on my way to the Citadel when I passed the ruins."

She gasped, as did a few others in the crowd that was gathering around him. Aeron looked at the faces. Most were feminine, with a few ancient men and some wide-eyed boys scattered amongst them. There was no one who readily seemed capable of -

Seinya?!

The face that emerged from the common house shook him. The shade of her chocolate hair, the hazel eyes, even her figure. All of it reminded him of Seinya. The only visible difference was the length of her hair, worn in a single long braid that reached her waist. *Seinya wouldn't be caught dead with a strand touching her shoulders,* he reminded himself.

The stablewoman spoke again. "You're going to the Citadel?"

"Yes. I'm headed there to finish my mastery rites and then return to the battlefield." He then turned toward the empty fort. "How many did Gaheris have with him?"

"Why do you want to know?" the stablewoman replied, her tone suspicious. Aeron glanced at her, wondering what had caused such a reaction. Then he felt the piercing eyes of the village on him.

Aeron smiled and said directly, "I'm a Sun Guard."

"Ha! A Sun Guard master at your age?" she jested as she pointed toward his hip. "Where is your sunsteel, then?"

Murmurs now swept through the crowd. Aeron noted that one face watched without speaking. It was the 'Seinya' girl, now flanked by two others who must have been her sisters. Aeron's gaze lingered on her, and she glanced away.

"Well?" the stablewoman asked.

Smirking, Aeron reached down and drew the sunsteel blade from his left hip. The crowd gasped as the light appeared from nowhere.

"What kind of Wraith magic is that?" the one-legged elder said in a gruff voice.

"It's a cloaking glamor," Aeron replied, "and many Sun Guards have learned how to use it while out east. A few can replicate the full cloak that the Wraiths wield, but I find cloaking one's gear is easier to maintain and simpler to explain when others see it." With that, he also shifted the glamor over his armor to show his allegiance to the Sun Guards. The sight sent waves of surprise through the crowd.

"You have to hurry!" the stablewoman exclaimed. "Gaheris said he needed everyone to face the Wraiths. If you ride now, you should be able to catch them."

Aeron held up a hand to calm her. "How long ago did they leave?"

"They left about three hours ago," the one-legged elder replied.

It didn't take more than a thought and a glance at the horizon to realize the problem with the request. Aeron shook his head. "I'll stay here."

"You're refusing to fight?" The stablewoman exclaimed before Aeron could speak. "Are you a coward?"

"Hardly." Aeron's voice held an edge to it from her insult. "If I were to ride now, I may not catch them before the battle begins. Even if I do, some Wraiths will split off to attack a village. My instincts say it will be this one. I will remain here to protect you."

"Why should we believe you?" the stablewoman asked.

"Kaylin," the one-legged elder started, but she spun on him.

"For all we know, he is a Wraith and trying to get us all together before he slaughters us."

"Why would you say that?" a melodic voice called.

Aeron turned to see the 'Seinya' girl turn away as all attention settled on her. *At least her voice is completely different,* he mused. She had the higher pitch of wonder and innocence, whereas Seinya had always possessed a darkly seductive voice.

Kaylin's screeches interrupted his thoughts. She was pointing to Snowstorm. "This is a Cambrian mare. Only a few of them can be found outside of Rigia."

"True," Aeron replied. "She was a gift from my first master."

"A likely story." Kaylin retorted.

"Enough," the elder said to her before motioning to Aeron. "Forgive her; both Gaheris and the hunter said to be wary of a scout coming into our midst."

Aeron bowed respectfully. "A wise response. I would be wary of myself too, if I had done the things I have." The reply got a few chuckles from the crowd.

"You say that some of the Wraiths will come for us?" the elder continued.

"I would bet on it, given my experiences with them."

"What should we do, then?" the elder motioned to the low sun. "There is not much time in the day, and few of us are capable of putting up a fight."

"Is there anywhere that can hide all of you? Then I will only need to defend one building instead of many."

The elder pointed behind Aeron. "The common house can fit the entire village and then some, but it has many entrances."

"What about the cellar?" another voice called.

Aeron didn't see who had said this, though judging from the 'Seinya' girl's face, it was one of her sisters. "What cellar?" he asked the elder.

"It's below the grain barn. We use it to store beer after the harvests. Mostly empty right now."

That's promising. "How easy is it to find the door?"

"Not very," Kaylin replied in a disdainful tone.

"She's right," the elder said. "The cellar is older than our village. Whoever built it put cobblestones over the hatch to match the floor. Unless you're looking for it, you wouldn't notice it."

"Sounds like a good place to hide," Aeron replied. "How quickly can you get a week's worth of provisions down there?"

"A week's worth?" Kaylin exclaimed. "Why that long?"

"If I fail, they might burn the village. You'll have to hide until the King can send a stronger force to dislodge them."

Kaylin started to protest, but the elder cut her off. "If you believe that's wise, we can do it." He then set his gaze on Kaylin. "It is no harm to move a few provisions for a little while."

She huffed, then started barking orders to the villagers. Aeron offered his help wherever he could, though he quickly found that his help was best appreciated away from Kaylin.

While he aided the villagers, Aeron also took every spare moment to strengthen the detection magic in his black blade. It wasn't long before he could sense

into the eastern trees when he focused on the energy.
I won't be surprised by any Wraiths tonight.

Several times he tried to approach the 'Seinya'
girl, but each time Kaylin called her away. Clearly the
stablewoman didn't trust Aeron, and by the look of
things, she didn't like the girl either. Every task
required a level of strength which the girl barely
possessed.

"Ivy," the voice of the stablewoman called
after Aeron's latest attempt at meeting the girl, "I need
you to carry the water barrels into the cellar."

Ivy. A nice, simple name.

Ivy gave her an annoyed look, then slowly
walked toward the common house.

Aeron cut in. "May I help you, Ivy?"

She spun around in surprise, then gave him a
brilliant smile. "Of course," she said and motioned for
him to follow her. Aeron cast a side-eye toward

Kaylin. She stood there in impotent fury for a few moments, then went to direct someone else.

Amused, Aeron walked over to help Ivy with the barrels. However, the amusement was short-lived as Aeron felt the energy of both blades leaching toward her. A simple mental spell stopped their calls to her. *She's a latent talent—and naturally attuned at that.*

There was protocol for such a thing. Aeron smiled at her. "Ready?"

She nodded, and the two lifted. The barrel yielded to his might, and he had to adjust his hold so that it didn't fall onto Ivy. "How's your grip?"

"Good," she replied. The two then carried the barrel into the cellar, with Aeron going down the stone stairs first to hold the bulk of the weight. After they set it down in the back, they repeated the process with the other two barrels. The work continued in relative silence as Aeron tried to imagine how the

Wraiths might act tonight. Ivy started to speak a couple of times, but she held her tongue before any words emerged.

As they finished moving the last barrel, Aeron decided to break the silence. "You're pretty strong."

"Thank you." She said with a touch of red on her cheeks, her eyes dancing away again.

"No need to be shy," he remarked.

She smiled softly. "I just... I noticed you keep looking at me."

"You remind me of someone I once knew." Aeron saw the disappointment strike Ivy instantly. He silently cursed his loose tongue and said, "She died three years ago, so it is strange seeing someone as beautiful as her again."

The red returned to Ivy's cheeks. This second remark seemed to please her. "How did she die?"

"Wraiths. I couldn't kill them in time to save her."

Ivy glanced away. "I'm sorry." After a few moments, her gaze turned to the east. "How could the Wraiths have gotten this far?"

He shook his head. "I don't know. We've done our best to contain them, but we are still mortal."

"You don't seem too afraid of them." Ivy said quietly, as though she had tried to stop herself from saying the words.

Aeron let his hard-fought confidence beam through his grin. "I'm not."

Ivy gave him a look. "But I've heard such terrible stories about them."

Dark thoughts sprang into his mind at the mention of Wraith atrocities. "I've seen what the Wraiths are capable of, so I would say to believe every story you've heard."

Her eyes widened. ". . . even what they do to prisoners?"

A sigh slipped out as Aeron remembered the horrors he'd witnessed. "Especially those stories."

Ivy looked at him fearfully. "What about the stories where a single Wraith kills twenty or more Sun Guards? They aren't that skilled, surely?"

"I've seen thirty fall to two Wraiths with my own eyes," he replied.

Her brow furrowed while she searched him for any sign that he was exaggerating. Aeron couldn't deny that attributing their foes with such a measure of skill was disheartening to anyone who would be opposing them, but the claim was no exaggeration.

The last time he'd witnessed such skill was the attack he'd mentioned, where thirty Sun Guards under Grand Master Melos had ambushed the Grand Inquisitor of the Wraiths, Micalus, and his apprentice during the Battle of Carkaroen. Aeron had been the only man to leave that encounter alive.

Still, Aeron knew Ivy needed something to inspire hope right now. He chuckled and said, "Even so, there are stories of the opposite. Arthur Duskling slayed two Wraiths with a sling back during the founding of the Sun Guards, and the last three years have taken many of the cult's best warriors."

"I've always liked the story of Arthur," Ivy said, a gleam of reverence in her eyes, "but he ambushed those ones. We're the ones being ambushed now."

"True, but I doubt the Wraiths would send their best so far away with all the losses they've had, and even with their skill, they only have a few ways to combat sunsteel." With that, he drew his blade and held it so Ivy could see its full profile. Aeron ran his fingers down the spine of the blade as if he were admiring it along with Ivy. He looked into her eyes. "Would you like to hold the blade?"

Her face did little to hide her surprise. "Me?"

Aeron nodded. "I see no reason to distrust you with it."

As Ivy took hold of the blade, it pulsed in a slow rhythm. She stared at the pulsing blade for a few moments, enamored by the rhythm. "Why is it doing that?" she asked.

"You have some latent talent," Aeron said as his other hand discreetly repeated the spell along the scabbard of the black blade. The pulse from it was more powerful. He felt his heart tighten. *The Wraiths will turn her if I cannot stop them.* He reached out to take the sunsteel back. "The Academy could train you in how to use your gift."

She handed him the blade, though it was a little while before she replied. "I don't know what to say."

He breathed a laugh. "You've never gone far beyond your village, have you?"

"No," she said, glancing away again. "My parents died before I can remember. Father took me and my sisters in, and the village has been my family ever since."

"I can understand. My parents died when I was young, too."

Her hazel eyes met his. "How did they die?"

"I never knew my father; I know my mother seduced him and then I know nothing but rumors after that. As for my mother, she was murdered when I was young. I became a warrior to avenge her death. I even trained under her best friend until Master Reylund took me in." Aeron shook his head at the memories and forced a breath of laughter to expel them. "What about your parents?"

"An illness took them both in the same week. Many died that spring."

"I'm sorry to hear that."

Ivy gave him a sad smile, then asked, "How long have you been in the east?"

This is my first time west of the Bicorun, but that would only confuse you. "I was at Redwood when the fighting started again."

Ivy's eyes went wide. "I heard nearly everyone died in that massacre."

"There were only a few survivors." Aeron replied with a heavy sigh.

"And you've been fighting ever since?"

He nodded.

"I take it you've faced the Wraiths many times?" the gruff voice of the one-legged elder asked. The two looked out to see that the townsfolk were starting to gather inside the grain barn. "Your distinct lack of concern leads me to believe that, at any rate."

Aeron nodded. "I have crossed blades with them too many times to count. Whatever legend you've heard of them, believe it."

The old man nodded solemnly, a haunting look in his greying eyes. "Believe me, I do."

Aeron straightened up, having seen that look numerous times during the last three years. "You fought them?"

The elder nodded. "Lost my leg to one of them. I was lucky; a group of Sun Guards swarmed him and cut him down, though they lost five of their own. I only survived because a healer was among their survivors."

Aeron shook his head in amazement. "I can't imagine facing one without magic."

"You're fortunate that you don't have to."

"What battle was it?"

The elder rubbed his chin. "It was during the Retreat from the Miras. They caught us a few miles east of the river in a clearing. Left a lot of good men on that side of the river. You young bucks are the first to have taken the far bank again."

Aeron nodded and glanced away. He had studied that battle many times during his youth. It had been the culmination of the Wraiths' great offensive under Micalus, then a newly minted and terrifying warrior. "That was a great loss for Arca. Many died that day."

"Aye. I lost more than a few friends in the fighting." The elder sighed. "We'd come so close to taking the Dreadfort only to get kicked all the way back across the Bicorun."

"I've heard that the slaughter was so great on both sides that the Wraiths themselves were the ones to offer peace." Aeron added.

The elder nodded. "It was a shock to everyone to hear that. We all believed old King Talos had offered the terms, but Melos insisted the Wraiths were behind it."

Aeron sat straight again at the casual mention of the former Grand Master. "You knew Melos?"

"He was from Birchwood, about a day's walk west of here. I knew his older brother growing up, so when Melos spoke, I knew he wasn't deceiving us."

A small boy piped up. "Why did the Wraiths give in? Weren't they winning?"

"I don't think we'll ever know," the elder replied. "Their ways are not natural."

That may be, but they already had their supposed key to victory after the battle. They just had to wait for it to mature. Aeron gave a heavy sigh. "If only that peace had lasted, but the Wraiths used the time to corrupt and train an entire generation for the war we fight now." Before anyone could get another word in, Aeron looked to the sky. "It's time to get everyone underground."

"Won't they see us?" Ivy asked.

He shook his head. "Wearing a full cloaking glamor requires both concentration and stamina.

They'll stay far out of sight until it's time for them to attack. How soon can we get everyone gathered?"

"Most of us are here now," the elder said. "There are a few who live out in the fields that haven't arrived yet."

"Get them here as quickly as you can," Aeron replied. "My instinct is that they will attack at sunset, or very soon after." Ivy left with her sisters and a few others to collect the stragglers. He turned to the gathered villagers and pointed into the cellar. "The rest of you get down there."

It was slow going, as some of the older women fought over bringing their treasured items with them and the children seemed to think it would be better if they gathered sticks and stones to help fight the Rigian force. It didn't help that Kaylin continued to question his motives, despite some strong words from the one-legged elder. Aeron found his patience tried more than once. *Is this what you have to deal with leading an army, Master Reylund?*

Ivy's sisters returned before half of the group had made their way down. Among the stragglers they brought was a bony lady who proved an immediate help. "Stop your nagging and get in the hole!"

"But Agnena," Kaylin said with pricked pride, "the Wraiths -"

"Would you rather face them up here in the open or down there where they only have one way in?! Don't be a fool. Get in the hole!" Kaylin hung her head and hurried into the cellar, as did many of the others who didn't want to catch Agnena's ire.

Aeron chuckled at the sight. "Thank you for that."

"Oh, don't worry about it. I'd rather we all went together, anyway." The remark caused Aeron to give the bony woman a look. She cackled. "Don't worry. The girls think you'll protect us just fine, and I'm inclined to trust their instincts."

"Speaking of," Aeron looked at Ivy's sisters, "where is Ivy?"

"Here," Ivy said as she appeared from around the corner, having armed herself with a bow. Her quiver held more arrows than most archers Aeron had met.

"Where did you find those?" he asked.

"The Hunter's Guild has a fletcher who lives here," she replied, a hint of pride hiding in her smile. "I've been practicing to join them."

Aeron smirked. "Well, hopefully you won't need those."

She nodded, then helped Aeron to usher in the other villagers. Soon, all but a few of the elderly remained above ground. Ivy glanced to the west. "The sun is setting."

It was a glorious sunset. The varied clouds burned red and gold against the darkening sky. "It's almost time." Aeron said quietly. He then reached out to help Agnena into the cellar.

"I hope they stopped the Wraiths before they cross the river," the bony lady stated as she slid underground. "The further away from us, the better."

"River?" Aeron asked. He had crossed no river during his trek, and no river had been in sight along the path the Wraiths would have taken to reach the village. His heart quivered. "Which way did your scouts say the Wraiths were coming from?"

"To the northeast," the one legged elder pointed, "by the broken peak."

Aeron tried to conceal his worry as he traced the courses on his mental map. It only confirmed his instincts. There was no means by which the Wraiths from last night had reached that point in one day.

They would have been even slower than he'd been with so many soldiers in their group.

That left only one reasonable conclusion.

"What's wrong?" Ivy asked.

Aeron shifted his eyes toward her. "I do not wish to cause undue alarm, but if your scouts are correct about their positioning, then there are at least two bands of Wraiths converging on us."

Murmurs swept through the cellar. He couldn't fault them. Eleven Wraiths were a terrifying force on its own, but upwards of twenty? He hadn't seen a roving band of Wraiths that large since the days before Carkaroen, and he had never known one so large to move this far from the Rigian army.

His eyes remained locked on Ivy. Although scared, she bravely put on a calming face. "Are you sure?" she asked.

Aeron leaned back against the stairs. "I should have asked before, but which way did that hunter go?"

Ivy looked to the elder, who slowly pointed to the east. "He remained behind to eat and rest after his ordeal. He left just before you arrived, saying that he would try to help the others if he could."

"Of course he did." Aeron shook his head and looked to the east. "He was a Rigian scout. Gaheris is marching right into a trap."

Small cries of agony rose from the villagers. Fear spread throughout the cellar, awakening the battle fever within Aeron. *I have to calm them, or the Wraiths will sense their fear as well.* He made a sharp whistle and silenced the crowd. "How strong is Gaheris' force?"

"Gaheris had two dozen Sun Guards and over a hundred regulars with him, as well as about forty from our village." The elder replied. "But if there are two bands, they will be outnumbered."

"Correct, but only against the Rigians." Aeron's mind was racing as he tried to think of how the Wraiths would react. The scout might have seen him and would add that to his report. If they had found their fallen comrade's ashes, they might dedicate more of their own to the village attack. "The Sun Guards will probably outnumber the Wraiths two-to-one. If Gaheris is as good a captain as you believe him to be, they might just stand a chance."

"But how many will you have to face?" asked Kaylin. "Can you really fight more than one at once?"

He laughed, hoping to relieve the tension. "As I told you, I'm going to complete my mastery rites at the Citadel. I have faced groups of Wraiths on my own before; you needn't worry about me." Yet even with the brave words, Aeron's concern grew about the battle facing him. *I could be up against ten. I haven't been outnumbered like that since Carkaroen, and I had help then.*

"How many Wraiths have you killed?" one of the little girls asked from inside the cellar. It took only a brief glance to see that the villagers had returned to the door to listen to the exchange.

Aeron opened his mouth to reply, but then decided a demonstration would hold far greater weight. "One moment." He then opened his shadow vault and took out one of the ritual daggers that he had transferred souls to. All idle talk ceased when the shadow vault opened, then soft whispers fluttered as he held out the dagger for all to see, its constellation of stars shifting gently and invitingly.

"What kind of blade is that?" Kaylin asked in a low voice that seemed instinctively aware of the dagger's sinister nature.

Aeron moved the blade around, taking care not to touch its edge. "It's the ritual dagger of a Wraith." Whispers of awe rippled at the revelation.

"What are those lights?" Agnena asked.

"Wraith souls that were sealed when the dagger stole their life force." Aeron replied. Murmurs quickly spread. Such a thing had likely never crossed their minds. The effect of the knowledge was immediate; Aeron felt the fears melt away as wonder took hold.

"I thought Wraiths can't kill each other?" the little girl asked.

Aeron laughed unexpectedly. "And who told you that?"

She pointed to the one-legged elder. "Grandfather told me."

"Did he now?" Aeron said as he crouched at the top of the stairs. Indulging the children would help the adults stay relaxed. "Well, he's right, for the most part. 'Wraiths can't kill Wraiths' is a well-known phrase in the east because they are immune to anything imbued with normal Wraith magic, and that magic protects them from many other magics. Their auras also keep most weapons from breaking their skin, though they will still feel the impact. That is why they are such feared fighters. They can strike without fear of harming their comrades during a battle."

"Wow!" The children said in awe.

"That would be amazing," a small boy added.

"No!" Aeron said in a fierce tone, quelling their excitement. "One advantage does not balance the atrocities that their order commits, and that fearlessness breeds recklessness. Just like how the Sun Guards rely on sunsteel, Wraiths rely on their magic. Negate that, and most panic."

"Why the dagger, then?" Ivy asked.

"Because Wraiths can kill Wraiths, given the right circumstances." Aeron stated as he put the dagger back into the vault before something went wrong, then forced a smile for the children. "The daggers are one of two major exceptions. They were crafted to seal a Wraith who betrays the order. Everyone in their cult carries a dagger like this, along with their chosen weapons, so that they can enact their own form of justice if needed. The magic of the blade absorbs the life force of the Wraith it strikes."

"Can it do that with anyone?" one of Ivy's sisters asked fearfully.

Aeron shook his head as he closed the vault. "It works in combination with the rituals to become a Wraith. Regular lives don't have that connection, therefore, it results in little more than a normal cut."

The elder leaned forward on his staff. "You mentioned two ways. What is the other?"

"Those are the Inquisitors' blades. They are nearly black, like the daggers or any weapon imbued with Wraith magic, but they also spark with lightning from a deeper magic. That magic instantly dispels any magic used by another Wraith, and many other magics as well, including sunsteel. They are the deadliest weapons known to man. Only the blade's master isn't at risk of injury from the blade, or whoever they choose to bind with it, such as their apprentice."

"Then they aren't all evil," the small boy said in a manner as though he had won an argument.

"Of course they are, Tristan!" several of the women exclaimed. The cellar devolved into chastising the boy for a while, with even the one-legged elder getting a harsh word in.

But as the voices died down, Ivy asked Aeron, "What do you think? Are they all evil?"

Aeron exhaled, thinking of Seinya and the few others after her who had been willing to turn before being struck down zealously. "I think many of them are misled, especially the younger ones who are merely following their elders. Their leaders, though, know full well what they do, and delight in it. And there's no denying that the ritual to become a Wraith is inhuman."

"What is it?" a voice asked.

"You don't want to know," Aeron replied, trying to keep his voice calm against the anger building within, "but once it's finished, a Wraith no longer bleeds and their body has altered such that when they die, they become ashes."

"Woah," all the children said.

"So, they're no longer human?" Ivy asked.

"To an extent," he said slowly, keeping old memories at bay. "All Wraiths were human at some point, and while they still appear human and act human, it is instilled in them that they have surpassed humanity once they've undergone the rituals." Thinking about the rituals further stirred his latent fury. "If there are any people in this world that approach pure evil, it is those who lead the Wraiths."

"They can't all be evil." Tristan remarked again. "The Wraithslayer left them and joined us."

Aeron smirked at the boy's rebuttal, and before he could form a response, the girl next to him said. "I would love to meet him."

"Have you ever met him?" another girl asked Aeron. The other children then clamored for him to answer, all caught up in childlike curiosity. Even some adults asked him excitedly about the man, one of them being Ivy.

The excited questions caused Aeron to smile. He'd never suspected that the name would generate such enthusiasm this far from the front.

The black blade pulsed at his hip. His mind snapped into focus instantly as he leapt to his feet. *Those stories will have to wait.* "They're here."

Part 3:

One Against Many

The murmuring started again. Aeron could only make out a few of the words. Mostly they expressed worries that the garrison had already fallen in battle. "Don't worry about Gaheris yet. This is always how the trap is sprung."

"How do you know the Wraiths so well?" Tristan asked, speaking for many of those gathered.

"You learn a lot in war," the one-legged elder replied grimly.

"If only it were that simple." Aeron said. He then turned to Ivy. "The moment I'm gone, shut and lock the door. Do not let anyone in. I don't care whose voice you hear, keep it locked and try to keep everyone quiet."

She nodded. "Do you have a sign that it is you, for when you come back for us?"

Aeron thought for a minute, then tapped a pattern on the cobblestones. "When you hear that, it's me. Otherwise, remain down here until you haven't heard any movement above for a full day." He then addressed the rest of the villagers. "Put out any lights and pray for a good outcome. Children, make sure your parents don't worry too much."

The children all agreed eagerly. With the villagers assured, Aeron turned to leave the grain barn.

"Won't they see you once you step outside?" Kaylin asked.

Aeron chuckled at her. "I don't think so." He then turned to Ivy as he channeled a glamor. "Ready?"

"Ready," she said. "Be safe, Aeron."

He smiled. "I can't promise that. I can promise that they won't harm you as long as I live."

She nodded to him, and Aeron saw the impetuous thought cross her mind. The cloaking glamor enveloped him as she leaned forward, and with the gasps of the villagers behind him, Aeron stepped away and tapped the pattern with his foot. After a few stunned seconds, Ivy shut the door. He then slipped into the shadow of a home and lowered the glamor before marching toward the Wraith energy.

The village faded around him as he focused his mind on the plan. His remaining glamors were ready to reveal his colors at a moment's notice. He just needed to be far enough from the village that none of the Wraiths from the primary group could sneak around him. Aeron would need to eliminate that group quickly enough that he could then hunt the flanking members before they could cause serious harm.

He could feel them now, their energy ranging from weak apprentices to warriors many years more versed than Aeron. In the dark, most eyes would have seen nothing, but Aeron knew what to look for. Coming from the trees were over a dozen shimmering shapes, like mirages on a hot day. They confirmed his suspicions. The merger of two raiding bands.

The shimmers were fanning out around him. Nine remained in view, while two more were flanking him on either side. Only Aeron's sense for magic allowed him to track the movements of those four.

Thirteen-to-one odds. Aeron chuckled at his luck. *Still better than Carkaroen.*

He held out a hand to signal the Wraiths. "Halt!"

The nine Wraiths he could see froze, while he felt the other four slow their pace to little more than a crawl. Even in their cloaked form, he could sense the interplay of surprise and curiosity.

Aeron smiled. He had gained the attention of both the primaries and the flankers; the first step of his plan lay completed as best as anyone could have hoped for.

The shimmers in front of him faded, with familiar figures taking their place. They wore black armor over their blood-red clothing, though only the middle two had steel breastplates. The rest appeared to wear the more traditional leather jerkins. That didn't mean they'd be easy to kill; when their protective aura became active, their leather would be harder to penetrate than ordinary steel. Their eyes glowed red behind the raven-like masks, save again for the two in the middle whose faces were bare. The last defining detail were the cloaks of black and red feathers, symbolizing the wings of death.

It was a terrifying visage.

Three were already shrouded in smoky auras, but the rest were not. These were relying on their passive auras. *Arrogance.* Aeron thought of this latter group. *Fools who believe themselves invincible.*

"Well, well. Looks like Reilynne's killer is an arrogant fool," one of the unmasked Wraiths said mockingly to his fellow.

"Be careful, Uhtred," the other unmasked one replied with an expressionless face, his aura fully developed around him. "Even a fool wouldn't be waiting for us so readily."

His aura is the strongest of the group. He's likely the leader of the entire raid, and Uhtred's his second-in-command. Aeron called out to the leader. "You will go no further."

Laughter rose from the other uncloaked cultists, Uhtred's being the most hearty. "And why do you believe that?"

"Call me a believer in destiny." Aeron kept his focus on tracking the four circling in on him. Their energy was similar to the apprentice from last night, Reilynne. Like her, they didn't suspect his skill. Instead, they were intent on getting the first kill of the night and avenging their fellow apprentice, while the others supposedly held Aeron's attention.

Sacrificial lambs.

"And what destiny is that?" the leader asked.

"To see the end of your kind," Aeron boasted. Again, his foes laughed, save for the leader, while the four were now nearly upon him. "Shall I demonstrate?" Aeron drew the sunsteel as he lunged toward the two on his right. Before they could power up their auras to resist the sunsteel's magic, Aeron's blade slipped past their guards and cut through their armor as if it were wax. The two corpses dissipated into ash as Aeron wheeled around.

The other two had dropped their cloaking glamors and were trying to charge their auras, but their steps were faltering. Aeron thought of using the dagger, but he held off. He needed to save his glamors for the third phase of his plan.

Both Wraiths were indeed young, proving no match for Aeron's hard-won skill. The sunsteel blade struck through the gaps in their armor and both fell into ashen heaps.

Nine more, but–

Aeron sensed a rippling energy lance toward him. He raised his sunsteel into a guard as he spun around to face his remaining foes. The purple bolt of energy dissipated against the sunsteel a moment before it would have struck his chest. That was no ordinary technique. Aeron's eyes darted around his remaining foes. *Which one of you can do that?*

What he saw caused a confident grin to spread over his face. Uhtred stared at him with his mouth agape, and of the other eight, only the leader had the same energy in his aura as when the fighting started; a few had even lost their auras altogether from their shock.

The leader, meanwhile, remained expressionless. *I'll assume it was you.*

"Your blade is indeed quick." The lead Wraith said before giving a banshee-like wail. The noise had its intended effect on his comrades as the cultists' auras returned to a readied state.

Aeron gave him a slight bow and laughed, giving the illusion of recklessness. *Now for the next part.* He then shifted into a ready position, the tip of his sunsteel aimed for the leader's heart. "I have had many exceptional masters to learn from in my brief life. Come and face your deaths against their skill."

"The quality of their instruction is clear," the Wraith said calmly, "but you have faced mere apprentices." He then turned to Uhtred. "The one who kills him will be commended to the Council."

Uhtred smiled eagerly, his aura growing larger as he let out his own wailing battle cry. "He will die, and there will be no one to remember his passing."

"Only if you kill his audience," said another Wraith with a wicked tone.

Aeron made a brief glance behind him. He found Ivy watching their fight from behind the nearest building and mentally cursed. *Now the Wraiths may target her as well.*

He returned his gaze to his foes, only to see a bolt of purple energy hurtling toward him, and all the Wraiths—except the leader—closing in, issuing their banshee-like calls. Aeron had watched many flee in the face of a single charging Wraith, let alone nine attacking at once. He took four slow steps backwards, noting that he would have Uhtred and two Wraiths to deal with immediately before the rest closed in.

No hiding it now.

Aeron answered them with his own banshee wail and surged forward. Uhtred stopped at once, his eyes wide in surprise. The other two took a few more steps before their charge faltered, but Aeron was upon them a moment later. He made a feint toward the first one he reached, then countered the other with a slash through the Wraith's face. The first Wraith slashed at Aeron's gut, but Aeron let the sword strike harmlessly against him while he thrust his sunsteel through the man's hip. The Wraith fell in a howl of pain.

Uhtred attacked before Aeron could bring his blade to bear. It was a perfect strike toward Aeron's unprotected head. All he could do was raise his arm into the blade's path and let fate take the lead.

The blade struck his open palm and stopped against a smoky aura.

Aeron gripped the blade and pulled down, taking Uhtred off balance. The sunsteel cut across Uhtred's throat before he could recover. The Wraith disintegrated into ash with wide eyes, disbelief turning to sheer astonishment as Aeron's glamors dispelled.

Tossing Uhtred's fading corpse aside, Aeron struck the killing blow to the wounded Wraith and turned to the remaining cultists.

Six.

They had stopped their charge to stare back at him, their auras distorted in stunned fury at what they saw. Everything that Aeron wore visually matched the lead Wraith, save for the white tunic beneath his armor and the Sun Guard's insignia stamped over the Wraith symbol on his breastplate. He even maintained the devilish glowing eyes to make sure there was no mistaking him for a costumed charlatan.

With a defiant smile, Aeron finally drew his black blade. Its sparks of lightning made clear what it was to his foes: the inquisitor sword of Micalus. It was the last thing they would need to identify him.

The third and final phase of his plan had sprung; all Aeron had to do now was survive the onslaught.

"Micalus' apprentice!" yelled the lead Wraith. The Wraith drew his own inquisitor's sword and rushed Aeron. "KILL HIM!"

The other Wraiths sheathed their swords and drew their daggers to follow their leader, their wails issuing once more from their ranks.

Aeron's heart skipped a beat. He hadn't planned for an Inquisitor to be among their ranks, especially once he hadn't seen the characteristic white mask. The only one of their number he'd ever slain was Micalus, despite the years of being hunted by the Wraiths. He had twice ambushed Inquisitors, but his companions had slain them before Aeron had the opportunity.

His scheme was based on the Wraiths switching to daggers once he revealed himself, giving him an advantage in reach. Not only did the Inquisitor's black blade pose a mortal threat to himself, but it was also a threat to his sunsteel. Such a foe would require far more focus for Aeron to survive, much less defeat.

There was no time to contemplate the surprise any further. *If I kill him now, the others will falter and be easy to pick off.* Aeron closed on the Inquisitor and struck with both weapons. The black blades sang off of each other, while the Inquisitor made a shield of energy around his free hand that deflected the sunsteel.

Startled, Aeron leapt back and narrowly avoided a stab from another Wraith. No new upstart could have used such magic so deftly. Micalus hadn't even begun instructing Aeron in that art when Aeron had killed him. It led to a chilling thought. *This Inquisitor must be a new member of the Council!*

The Inquisitor struck again. Aeron spun from this attack and slashed his black blade at another Wraith. It barely caught the man's jerkin, which hissed as the protective aura was momentarily dispelled by the deeper magic woven within the blade. The sunsteel followed a moment later. With nothing to negate the sunsteel's magic, it cleaved through the jerkin and eliminated one more foe.

The black blade sang again against the Inquisitor's. Aeron retreated a step and felt a dagger bounce off his pauldron, having barely missed his neck. He struck with the sunsteel at his attacker, scoring a hit to the Wraith's exposed arm. Aeron didn't know how deep the wound was, but he knew he'd hit flesh by the shimmer that flashed over the man's skin.

The Inquisitor was pressing in. Aeron countered the next few strikes skillfully, but he likewise couldn't land a hit on the man. The other Wraiths were circling around the two, looking for their chance to be the one to slay Aeron.

Aeron took a risk and spun past the Inquisitor. Two Wraiths were waiting on the other side. All four fighters struck at once. The daggers of the two Wraiths barely missed Aeron's joints as he leapt into the air. Aeron's sunsteel caught one Wraith beneath the chin while the black blade cracked against the other's armor, and the Inquisitor struck Aeron across the back.

His armor hissing, Aeron wheeled to deflect the Inquisitor's killing blow while the sunsteel cut clean through the now unprotected Wraith.

Three.

Once more the Inquisitor pressed his attack, and the remaining Wraiths' daggers kept clinking against Aeron's armor as he desperately held his ground.

One Wraith suddenly lurched and gave a small cry. Aeron saw an opening and drove the sunsteel into the Wraith's waist just below his jerkin. The black blades again sang against each other as Aeron retreated a step.

Two.

He caught the glint of something sailing past, but he paid little mind to it as he charged. Aeron focused his attacks on the Inquisitor, waiting for the man to make one misstep in his defense.

A dagger again sounded against Aeron's pauldron, but the Inquisitor held his ground.

The other Wraith gave a cry of pain, and when Aeron cast a quick glance in his direction, he saw it was the one he'd cut earlier. The Wraith looked to be disintegrating.

The glance nearly cost Aeron his life as the Inquisitor struck at his neck, but Aeron ducked his head and lifted his shoulder. The pauldron rose just enough to deflect the strike upwards, hissing as its protective magic was now gone.

Aeron leapt back and glanced around again. Sure enough, the other Wraith was gone. The glint from earlier came to mind. *Was that an arrowhead?*

The Inquisitor paid Aeron's supportive ally no heed, his anger fully focused on his prey. "You have defiled your master's blade," The Inquisitor exclaimed in a cold fury as he renewed his attack. "How could you betray our Oath?"

Aeron blocked the incoming strikes. "Because I realized the Oath and the Order are evil."

"Says the one who killed his master in cold blood!"

"We've murdered thousands more in cold blood, not to mention how many you and the others have forced into the Order."

The red eyes flared. "Your heresy ends now!" The Inquisitor maneuvered his blade past Aeron's guard and barely connected with the sunsteel blade. Its radiance faded instantly, just what Aeron had been trying to avoid.

Though the sunsteel's magic had momentarily dispelled, the Inquisitor had reached too far to gain the advantage. Aeron responded by striking the pommel of the sunsteel against the Inquisitor's head, then slashed with the black blade. Even though he'd been stunned by the first blow, the Inquisitor's instincts carried him almost out of reach of the slash.

The Inquisitor staggered back, somehow keeping his footing. A thin line of ashy flesh ran along the man's temple from where the blade had given a glancing cut, but it was the Inquisitor's eyes that Aeron focused on. Their glow was wild. Fanatic.

Aeron tossed the dimmed sunsteel away and took a moment to reach out and feel if the remaining Wraiths had arrived. He felt nothing. The other group was likely still being held up by Gaheris's force. He gripped the black blade tighter and surged for his final attack. *If I can land the killing blow now . . .*

Their blades sang for a few moments before a blast struck Aeron in his chest. The Inquisitor had slyly formed another energy bolt and used it on Aeron's still-recovering armor, punching right through the Sun Guard insignia.

The sudden impact thrust Aeron back violently. He landed with a grunt, causing him to lose his grip on the black blade. His body went limp, one hand on the hole in his armor, the other by his hip.

"Your heresy is finished." Aeron heard through the pain. His mind was trying to make sense of what he felt. *Does this mean the wound is fatal?* He closed his eyes and took a deep breath. The numbness from the hole was spreading, as if coursing through his veins.

When Aeron opened his eyes again, the Inquisitor was standing over him. "You were a fool to hesitate," the Inquisitor said smugly as he readied the killing blow. "Now this village will run red with the blood of those you couldn't save."

At that moment, an arrow struck harmlessly against the Inquisitor's chest. The man turned his gaze to the impertinent archer, and Aeron made one last desperate attack. Despite the numbness, his hand clutched the Wraith dagger at his hip as he kicked at the knee of the Inquisitor. The knee buckled, and the Inquisitor swung his blade in retaliation.

Aeron barely rolled clear of the slash, drawing his dagger from its sheath as he did. Aeron saw the

Inquisitor form another bolt in his hand. He threw the Wraith dagger just as the bolt lanced toward him.

The force of the blast threw Aeron across the ground, leaving him breathless when he finally stopped with his face toward the sky. All feeling below his neck had vanished. He tucked his chin and saw the Inquisitor had fallen as well, Aeron's dagger deep in the disintegrating face. Aeron held on to consciousness for a few seconds more before he slipped into darkness.

Part 4:

A New Guard

The first thing Aeron noticed was that his chest was throbbing and a damp rag lay across his forehead. A groan escaped without his permission.

"Easy, Aeron," came a voice. In his daze, it sounded like Seinya's.

He opened his eyes to see that he was lying on a bed in a small room. His gaze pointed toward an open window. The light, mixed with the warm air, told him it was already evening again.

The damp rag shifted under an unseen hand. He turned to see Ivy's caring smile. "I take it we won?" he asked with a wince. Even speaking was painful.

"Yes," she replied, her motherly tone close to what Seinya would sound like after a battle. "You should have seen Tobin's reaction to your cloaking glamor. He immediately called you a Wraith once he got his voice back, then said you must be the Wraithslayer. Agnena was still mocking Kaylin about it when I left to follow you."

"That was a brave thing to do," Aeron whispered in order to mitigate the pain. "Without your arrows, I would have died."

She smiled sheepishly. "I only wish I had thought to attack them sooner."

"The arrows served their purpose, and you even killed one of them." He fought to ignore the throbbing as he joked, "That means that you could be called Ivy Wraithslayer now."

"I suppose it does, Wraithslayer," she said. Aeron smiled when her cheeks turned red as she realized the implication of them both carrying the same name.

He turned the subject to spare her more embarrassment. "What of Gaheris and his men?"

"They were able to overcome the ambush," she said and gave a heavy sigh. "A lot of people died, but the Wraiths and Rigians have fled."

"There are still Wraiths left?" Aeron tried to ignore the pain as his body tensed for another fight. He was vulnerable in this place. *If there are more, I have to be moving. For all our sakes.*

"The other Sun Guards are out looking for them." Ivy placed a gentle hand on his shoulder. "Gaheris believes there are still two hiding somewhere. He said that he counted twenty-two ashen heaps between their battle and yours."

The sigh of relief which escaped Aeron's chest felt soothing. "Good."

Ivy tilted her head in confusion. "Why?"

"One of their number died on the other side of the hills, and I killed a second as I was making camp the other night. That's the twenty-four Wraiths accounted for."

"They'll be glad to hear that." The smile Ivy gave seemed to warm Aeron's soul. "What will you do now?"

"Once I'm healed, I'll leave. I need to complete the rites at the Citadel and return to the front, both for my protection and for the good of the realm."

"Why the good of the realm?" she asked.

"Remember what I said about the Wraith hunting down traitors? They won't stop until I'm dead, and the further I am from them, the more innocent lives will be caught between us. On the battlefield, I needn't worry so much. Here, they can cause harm to many while they hunt for me."

"I understand." Ivy nodded as her hands checked his bandages. "What about when the war is over?"

Aeron glanced away, words failing him. *I never really thought that far ahead.*

Soft laughter from Ivy brought him out of his thoughts. "You have only known the battlefield, haven't you?" she asked.

He nodded. "Almost my entire life."

Ivy looked at him for a moment, as if unsure of what she was about to say. Then a mischievous smile turned her lips. "If you'd like, after the fighting is done, I can teach you about life outside of the battlefield."

The offer both surprised and intrigued him. He quickly thought of excuses and half-truths to refuse it, but he held them at bay. Sure, there would be far more women in the capital that would be a better match for his Duskling lineage, but how many of them could fight alongside him? *She's already seen how Wraiths fight and has heard the battle cry. That gives her an advantage over anyone, even many who've trained at the Citadel.*

The thought reminded him of the test he'd given her. "The sunsteel wasn't the only blade that called to you."

She looked confused for a moment, then her eyes widened and she turned to where the black blade rested against the wall. "You mean . . . they may make me one of them?"

"Normally, yes. However, the knowledge that you helped kill an Inquisitor might spare you from that fate if they ever come here again." Aeron sighed. "That said, they may try to turn you to spite me. You wouldn't be the first Wraith created for such purposes."

Ivy stood up and looked out the window. Aeron held his tongue as she pondered her own desires. It was not a simple choice for anyone. "Will I be with you?" she asked finally, her gaze settling on him again.

He let out a slow breath. "I would like that, but that is for others to decide. I have my own training to undergo, which will be of a much different nature than what yours would be."

There was silence for a moment. "I knew that would be the case," she said, "but my heart says this is the right thing to do, too." She walked back over and sat beside him. "If nothing else, leaving here may protect my sisters from their retaliation. When will you leave?"

Aeron let out a coarse laugh, his chest still pained by the sudden movements. "Once I can get to my feet again without collapsing. How long do you think that will be?"

"Not long, if I have anything to say about it." Ivy smiled and adjusted the bandages around his chest. "Though it is strange to see wounds with no blood."

Aeron grinned, knowing what the inside of his wounds looked like. Blood still coursed through his veins, but Wraith blood turned to ashes when exposed to air. "The ashening flesh still heals like normal, so long as the wounds are closed."

"That's what Gaheris told me." She let out a sigh and turned her hazel eyes toward his. "I think you should rest for a few days. See how the peaceful life feels for a change."

Aeron smiled at her, then pushed himself into a seated position. Ivy sat back to give him space. He could feel the lingering effects of the attack. The pain seemed to course through his body with every beat of his heart, as though his very blood had been the target of the Inquisitor's blast. Maybe it had been. Micalus had many abilities that were beyond Aeron's understanding; perhaps this was one Aeron would have learned before his betrayal at Carkaroen changed his fate.

He was sitting now and it pleased him to find that, despite all the pain, he wasn't lightheaded. So long as he was in a state where he wouldn't faint, Snowstorm could get him to the Citadel safely. Aeron turned to Ivy. "How many days?"

Ivy glanced between his eyes and the wound in his chest. When she spoke, it was softly stern. "Rest through tomorrow, then we can leave."

"Very well. Let Gaheris know of my intentions, and to not worry about any more Wraiths."

Aeron watched Ivy turn to leave, noting the sparkle in her eyes at the sudden change in her life's fortune. He wondered if his eyes had ever been like that at some point, either when he was first accepted into the Wraiths or when the Sun Guards had taken him into their ranks. The former hadn't been a surprise, but had given him a purpose: to kill his mother's murderers. The latter had followed the revelation of who his father's family was and had been a chance to atone for his own monstrous actions.

A thought struck him. "But first,"

Ivy stopped in the doorway. "Yes?"

"Where is my dagger?"

She turned and reached down beside the black blade. Aeron gingerly shifted himself to see what was there.

"We put all of your things here," Ivy said gently, as if dissuading him from moving more than he had to. "Gaheris took the gear from the last Wraith you killed and sent it to the Citadel, along with word of your victory." She then handed him the dagger and left the room.

Aeron waited until he was sure Ivy was gone before he fought his way to his feet. He staggered slightly, but his legs still moved like they should. The pain was slowly becoming a part of him now. A new constant companion until he could get someone at the Citadel to purge his body.

Maybe that knowledge could hold the key to cleansing the Wraith souls he carried with him.

Exhaling, Aeron unsheathed the dagger. He immediately knew which of the lights was the Inquisitor's. Never had he seen one so large, nor had he seen one crisscrossed with black sparks. The soul was like the inverse of the inquisitor blades.

Aeron could also feel the latent energy that the dagger now held. It called to him, to his Wraith side...

He quickly sheathed the dagger and set it back with the rest of his gear. Aeron silently swore that he would transfer the Inquisitor's soul to its own dagger as soon as he healed enough to perform the transfer.

There was danger in the melody of that power. Even with their body destroyed, the Inquisitor was currently the greatest threat to Aeron.

His thoughts tracked westward, picturing the grand building that lay at the end of his current journey. All those years ago, he dreamed of conquering the Citadel alongside Micalus and Seinya. Now, that place was the heart of his quest for redemption.

I wonder what awaits at the Citadel? Aeron settled back into the mattress and closed his eyes. Then, for the first time in years, he fell into a deep sleep.

END

Pronunciation Guide:

<u>People:</u>

Aeron Duskling (Air-un Duhsk-ling)

Agnena (Ag-nee-nuh)

Arthur Duskling (Ar-ther Duhsk-ling)

Gaheris (Guh-hair-ehss)

Ivy (Eye-vee)

Kaylin (Kay-lin)

Melos (Meh-lowss)

Micalus (Mih-kay-luhs)

Reylund (Ray-lund)

Seinya (Sayne-yuh)

Tobin (Toe-bin)

Uhtred (Ooh-tread)

<u>Locations:</u>

Arca (Ar-cah)

Bicorun (Bih-core-uhn)

Cambria (Cam-bree-uh)

Carkaroen (Car-car-own)

Miras (Mee-rahss)

Redwood (Rehd-wuhd)

Rigia (Rih-ghee-uh)

Afterword:

Thank you for reading *Wraith*. I hope you enjoyed Aeron's tale. If you have any feedback, I would appreciate hearing it so I can improve my writing in future projects — both regarding Aeron and in the other tales I hope to weave.

The original idea for *Wraith* took shape in January of 2020 (thank you Google Docs for timestamping everything automatically). That outline is quite different from what you've just read, focusing on Aeron meeting with the Sun Guard Masters before he is sent to the Citadel. From there, I built out the tale to where we stopped here.

Once I committed to being an author in 2024, I shopped *Wraith* to various literary magazines with the intent to build up funds for later endeavors.

It went a bit long on the timeline (literary magazines are a very competitive market) and I was told to cut the original opening to streamline the tale in my last rejection letter.

After doing so, I caught the eye of the staff at Sally Port Magazine. They provided great help in redrafting the beginning of second act and were a joy to work with. *Wraith* is far better because of their willingness to take me in and show what improvements would best benefit the story.

I can honestly say Aeron has become one of my favorite characters I've created. The powers of the Wraiths are fun to utilize, including ones not yet seen; however, it is Aeron's quest for redemption in particular — both for himself and the perhaps forlorn hope for the other Wraiths — which keeps me coming back.

Here I should acknowledge the clear opening for a sequel, and I have outlined such a venture. There must be caution in expecting a sequel any time soon. Firstly, I am committed to finishing *The Hammer of Fate* series over the next couple of years. Secondly, as much as I enjoy Aeron as a character, I hate going into Wraith culture for any great length of time. They are a twisted sort, and much of my exploration of this world has gone to Aeron's days as a Wraith since his turn to the light is so central to the narrative.

So, while I do want to eventually write the downfall of the Wraiths by Aeron's hand and the hands of his allies, it will be a while before I complete it. My apologies if this is upsetting, but I don't want to rush a story with such dark elements.

Acknowledgements:

There are several groups of people who I would like to thank for getting *Wraith* completed.

Thank you to Elijah, Eliana, and my mother for providing insight in the drafting phases of this tale and catching the many issues I wrote in the early days.

Thank you to Patrick, Nate, and everyone else at Sally Port Magazine for taking a chance on *Wraith* and helping me craft it into the state it is today. So much of the story would have never existed without your critiques and editing prowess.

Most importantly, I would be remiss to not point to God and the hope of redemption all of us have in the sacrifice and resurrection of His son, Jesus Christ. There is no heart He can't change, if only you will turn to Him.

Until next time. Take care, and may God bless you in the days ahead.